SMOKE

BLESSING MONTANA: BOOK ONE

MARISSA DOBSON

Published by Dobson Ink
Printed in the United States of America
ISBN-13: 978-1-946474-19-3

ACKNOWLEDGEMENT

I would like to take a moment to thank everyone who helped me make *Smoke* happen.

Smoke was previously titled *Through Smoke* and was published as part of Paige Tyler's Dallas Fire and Rescue Kindle Worlds. First, I would like to thank Paige for allowing me to be part of such a wonderful experience. Second, if you haven't checked Paige's books out yet, please be sure you do. You won't regret it.

I decided to do some rewrites before republishing *Smoke*. As much as I enjoyed being part of Paige's world, I've decided to remove the Dallas Fire and Rescue world. Instead of taking place in Dallas, *Smoke* has been reworked to fit into one of my already existing series, Blessing, Montana.

Originally, I had planned a second book, *Fire*, featuring Smoke's brother, Fire, which I ended up putting on the back burner. However, I'm pleased to announce *Fire* is now complete and will be available soon.

I would like to thank the men and women who put their lives on the line every day to do their job. First responders—police officers, firefighters, EMTs, and paramedics—deserve our gratitude. Their sacrifices are great in order for them to get the job done. Thank you. To my family and friends who are firefighters, thank you for taking the time to answer my questions. If I made any mistakes in *Smoke,* they are mine and mine alone.

With every book there is a whole team who work together to produce the final piece. Without my critique partner, as well as my editing and proofing team, the book wouldn't shine as it does. Thank you, Brynna Curry, for working this book into your schedule even with my tight deadline and your amazing turn around. Also thank you Kellie Montgomery for stepping in to edit *Smoke* when I needed someone with an opening in their schedule.

Last but certainly not least, I would like to thank my amazing husband, Thomas. Those of you who read the dedications and acknowledgements in my books will see that he's mentioned in each of them. That's because he's my biggest supporter. I don't know if I would have ever published my first book without him. He's incredible and I couldn't have asked for a better soulmate. I love you, Thomas.

CHAPTER ONE
BREAKDOWN

"Don't do this. Not now!" Monica Robinson slammed her hand down on the steering wheel, cursing her car. She looked down at the gauges, unable to believe what she was reading. *Out of gas.* She tapped the dashboard, as if that was going to send the needle away from the red E and start the car. *I just filled up this morning on the way to work.* She grabbed her purse and dug into the side pocket for her cell phone. Pulling it out, she hit the power button to wake it up but the screen remained black.

"Fuck." She leaned forward, resting her head on the steering wheel. A dead cell phone battery was the last thing she needed right now. She just wanted to go home. It had been a long day and after dealing with three spoiled brats and then spending hours at the police station, she was dead on her feet. Her string of bad luck was growing worse with every second and her patience was gone. Between her asshole ex-roommate, Sheila Price, and her own bad luck, it was the makings of a disastrous combination.

Stranded on a dark road with little to no traffic during the day, let alone at nearly one in the morning, with no cell phone and a dead car, left her few options. She'd have to leave her car there and walk, otherwise she would be there until morning when someone might stumble upon her car on the side of the road. As tired as she was, walking sounded like a better idea than spending the night in her car. It was a safe area but with Sheila out for blood, she couldn't take the chance. Renting a remote house near Blessing, Montana seemed like the perfect idea at the time. It would get her away from her lunatic ex-roommate and after growing up in the country this is where she felt at home. She needed peace and quiet. This place kept her close to town, without having to live in the mix of busybody neighbors. *Doesn't seem like such a great idea now.*

She dropped the useless phone back into her purse and pulled the keys from the ignition. Two miles was nothing, but in the dead of night, it didn't sound very appealing. She had no idea what might be lurking in the woods, but if her luck continued to run as it had, she wouldn't be surprised to find Sheila waiting to attack her. Or even a bear. She had been doing her best to keep her new address quiet but news traveled fast in small towns like Blessing. She could only hope since Sheila lived in the next town over it hadn't made it to her yet.

Opening her car door with the small flashlight she kept in the driver's door compartment in hand, she stepped out into the humid air. Summer was in full swing but it wouldn't be long until the chill of winter was in the air. An owl echoed in the distance and a longing to go home overwhelmed her. Maybe she had made the wrong decision moving away from everything she knew. A country girl from South Dakota who grew up on a farm her whole life, she had wanted something different. Blessing, Montana was supposed to be her chance to escape her small town and spread her wings, only it didn't turn out like she planned.

Before she made the move, she accepted a job as a nanny for a well-to-do family just a short drive outside of Blessing. After years of helping her mother with her seven younger siblings, three children should have been a walk in the park for her, but she hated it. Spoiled rich kids whose parents were never around. Making up for their absence by lavishing them with gifts was just too much for her. When she accepted the job, she thought it would be like it had been with her siblings. She never expected to hate every minute she spent with her charges.

She could go back home to South Dakota; her family would welcome her with open arms, but it wasn't what she wanted. Her parents respected her need to spread her wings, but at the same time urged her to come back home. She was the eldest of eight girls and her father was counting on her to meet a nice country boy, settle down, and take over the family farm. If she didn't it would be up to her younger sisters to marry someone who could take over the farm, otherwise they'd lose it when Dad could no longer carry on doing the work himself. Her father was old fashioned and didn't want his girls running the farm, their places were making a home for their husbands and raising the children, not out tending to the land and feeding the cattle each day.

"I want more than to just be a wife and mother." She kicked the dirt road, sending dust through the air. Demanding careers like Mr. and Mrs. Day had wasn't what she wanted either. Careers like that put too much strain on their marriage and took their time away from the kids. When she had children, she wanted to be there for them, just like her mother had been. Somewhere in the mess of her emotions, she knew there was a fine balance, one that would allow her to be more than just a wife and a mother but would still give her what she needed to be happy.

"Hey…" Jumping back in fear, she stumbled on a rock, nearly losing her balance. "Hey now, be careful."

Getting her feet under her she looked at the man behind the wheel of the truck. She had been so lost in her thoughts she hadn't heard the truck ramble up the dark road. The dangers of that weren't something she wanted to consider, at least on the side of the road in the middle of the night. "Sorry, I didn't…" She let the words die on her lips. How big of an idiot did she have to be to admit she didn't hear the engine of his truck coming down the road?

"Was that your car about a half mile back?" He tipped his head toward the side, indicating the car somewhere lost in the sea of blackness.

Half mile? That's how far I've gotten? "Yeah."

"Want me to look at it?"

She shook her head and stepped closer to the passenger door of the truck so she didn't have to holler over the engine. "Thanks, but it's not worth it. It's out of gas."

"Well hop in and we'll go get you some."

"I really appreciate the offer but—"

He gripped the steering wheel and rose off the seat, pulling his wallet from the back pocket of his jeans. "Trust me. I'm a safer bet than walking alone out here at this time of night. I'm a firefighter with Blessing Fire and Rescue, and we're neighbors. I saw you moving in last week as I was about to head out for my shift." He held the identification card out to her.

She looked at the ID he held out to her and nodded. "No gas, but I'd appreciate the lift home. If we're neighbors it shouldn't be out of your way. By the way, I'm Monica Robinson. It's nice to finally meet my only neighbor."

"You too, now hop in and let's get out of this heat."

Opening the passenger door, the dome light illuminated him, giving her a better look at his features. Short brown hair, falling every which way, and amber brown eyes that held a hint of darkness as if he had seen too much. His handsome face was chiseled with details, and she had no doubt the body hidden behind the jeans and dark blue pullover would be toned to match. His dark tan reminded her of home and someone who worked outdoors.

"It's really no problem to go get you gas." He offered again as she stood holding the passenger door open.

"Actually it is." Without taking her gaze from him she climbed into the passenger seat. "Someone cut my gas line."

"Are you sure?" he asked, raising an eyebrow at her.

She kept her hand on the door, not sure if she should be insulted or not. Before her dad would even allow her to go for her permit to drive she had to pass his test. At the time she thought it was a lot of useless knowledge about cars that she'd never need, but over the years she realized what a valuable lesson he gave her. She wasn't a mechanic by any means but she could diagnose the main issues with a car, as well as change her own oil and a flat tire.

"Yes, I'm sure. I might be a woman, but I know a thing or two about cars. I put gas in the tank this morning and now it's empty." Closing the door, she shook her head. She was in this mess because she was too trusting, but she didn't need to take it out on him. "I'm sorry. It's been a long day. I shouldn't have snapped at you."

"I have a buddy who can swing by in the morning with his tow truck and take it to his shop to fix it."

"Thanks, but you've already gone out of your way to help me. I can call around in the morning and find someone." He put the truck in drive and took his foot off the brake as she sat there wondering what she was going to do about Sheila. Would she get rid of her if she moved back to South Dakota? Or would she follow her? The idea of the lunatic following her home and endangering her parents and younger sisters terrified her. Going back home wouldn't be an option until something stopped Sheila. "Who knows what else is wrong with it? That bitch probably did as much to it as she could."

"Who?"

"Sheila Price. I rented a room from her before I found out that she's certified insane. As in she deserves to be locked up. The cops know who she is and they've had run ins with her before, but there's not much evidence. Maybe this was the break that we needed." At the end of the road her small cabin came into view. A welcome sight after the day she'd been through. "She would have had to cut the gas line when I was at the police station. I parked a

7

block away in the grocery store lot because I knew there'd be cameras and because I planned on picking up dinner on my way home. Instead, I was there for hours and now I just want to go to bed."

"I'm sorry to ruin your plans, sleep needs to wait a bit longer; you need to give the police a call. Have them check the security cameras and I'll get my friend out here because I suspect you're right about the fuel line. There was a trail leading up the road, getting lighter the closer I got to your car and now there's nothing. They might check the car for fingerprints. I don't know. It's not my line of work, but I know they'll do whatever they can to get her behind bars if she's terrorizing you." He pulled up the driveway and right out front of her house. "Go on in. I'll wait until the police arrive, just in case."

"Could I…" She shifted uncomfortably in the seat and turned toward him. "You've already done so much for me, and I truly appreciate it, but I need one more thing. My cell's dead and I never got a house phone."

"Here." With a grin he held out his phone.

"What a great impression I'm making." She shook her head again, sending her dark brown hair flying into her face. "I swear I'm not some drama freak. I moved out here to get away from her. I knew staying in town would make it too easy for her to find me. Last thing I want to do is bring this insanity to my neighbors' doorsteps."

"You haven't and neighbors help each other. If there's anything I can do, I'm right over there." He pointed to a large country home on the other side of the tree line separating their properties. "I'll be off for the next forty-eight hours; if you need anything at all, come on over."

"Forty-eight hours? That's an odd way of putting it, isn't it? I don't know many who'd word it like that. Most would say two days."

"Firefighters aren't most people." He gave her a quick, cocky grin. "Actually, it's because we're on for twenty-four hours and then off for forty-eight."

"Oh and here I thought it might be a Montana thing." She dug through her purse, looking for Detective Wilson's business card. The name on the ID her rescuer had shown her earlier popped back into her thoughts. "Wilson?"

"Excuse me?"

"Smoke Wilson, are you related to Detective Wilson?" She pulled the card from the back of her wallet and looked down at the name. "Detective Blaze Wilson."

"Well now. I know you're in good hands if he's the one assigned to your case." He reached over, hit the contact button, and scrolled down to the name Blaze, bringing his number up on the screen. "My brother, the only one who didn't follow in our father's footsteps and become a firefighter. Give him a call."

"It's a different number."

"Don't worry. It's his private cell phone, but he's sure to answer that. Considering he's been off duty for twenty minutes now, it's the only chance you have of speaking with him tonight. Otherwise the number you have will go straight to voicemail." He pushed Blaze's number before she could argue, giving her no other option but to put the phone to her ear.

Please let him help…

CHAPTER TWO
INVESTIGATION

Smoke watched the brown haired beauty as she spoke with Blaze. Her sweet accent had enticed him; he wanted to hear her talk more. He wanted to hear the way she'd laugh and overall he wanted to get to know her better. She lit something within him that he thought had been extinguished long ago. But it was the fear radiating from her as she told Blaze of her suspicions about Sheila and the fuel line that made him want to protect her. Unlike most women he met, she wasn't trying to put on a damsel in distress act. Whatever was happening between her and Sheila had her frightened. She tried to hide it with annoyance and anger but she couldn't keep the fear out of her eyes. The last thing he needed to do was get tangled up with his new neighbor and a possible lunatic but he couldn't very well stand by and do nothing.

"He wants to speak with you." She held the phone out to him.

"Don't worry. He's the best." He took the phone from her and brought it to his ear. "You coming over or what?"

"Wait, let's discuss what I just overheard. I'm the best, huh?" Blaze let out a deep laugh.

"Don't let it go to your head. Now what's your plan?" He didn't mean to sound short but after the twenty-four hours he had on duty he was ready to drop into his own bed and sleep for at least eight hours if not more. Call after

11

call had made the shift go by in a flash but had also left him exhausted. Even for the summer months with the search and rescue calls coming in for lost hikers it had been an unusual shift. He expected the longer hours in the winter with car accidents and chimney fires, but not on a beautiful summer day.

"I'll get T-Bone to load it onto his flat bed and then I'll meet him at his shop to look it over. I'll get a warrant for the security videos and we'll see what we find. Meanwhile, I want you to give her this number and since you're closer, give her yours. I know I'm asking a lot, but Sheila Price is dangerous. Out in the woods where you guys live, you're closer than any emergency personnel."

"Don't worry, Blaze." He glanced at Monica, whose brows were knitted together in confusion. "I'm off for forty-eight so I'll be around. Give me a call if you need me for anything."

"Get some rest." With that, Blaze ended the call. With things in motion, Smoke turned his attention back to the woman who needed the same confirmation.

"Blaze will take care of your car but if the security camera shows her tampering with it they might need time to process it. Do you need a ride to work tomorrow? Well, I guess it's already tomorrow."

For a long moment before answering him she stared out at her cabin. For a moment he wondered if she was debating how much she wanted to trust him. The downturn of her lips gave him the insight it might be deeper than that. What else was going on with her? Surely the sadness radiating off her wasn't just from the issues with Sheila. The fear he could understand but the unwavering sadness left him questioning what more was happening.

"Thanks but I'm off tomorrow; actually I'm off for the next few days. Possibly soon to be out of a job."

"Don't be so rough on yourself. Blaze is the best, he'll get to the bottom of this, and I'm sure your boss will understand."

"Doubt that." She let out a deep sigh full of regret. "I'm a nanny. Once they find out what's going on they'll have no choice but to let me go. Not that I could even blame them. Who would want someone watching over their child who brought danger to their doorsteps?"

He pulled down the visor and removed a piece of paper before quickly jotting down the numbers and handing it to her. "This is my cell number and the second one is for Blaze. If you need anything, give me a call."

She took the paper he held out to her and opened the door. "Thanks. To express my gratitude how about I cook dinner for you. Tonight, say seven?"

"You don't have—"

"I want to." She climbed out of the truck and looked back at him. "What do you say? Dinner?"

"A home cooked meal sounds pretty amazing. It's been a while since I had one that wasn't at the station. So yeah, I'll be here. Anything I can bring?"

"If you drink beer or wine you might want to bring some. Just moving in and not entertaining much, so I don't have any on hand and without a car…well you know." She slung her purse over her shoulder. "I'll see you tonight."

"See you tonight." He nodded as she shut the door.

He waited until she made it inside and the living room light switched on before he pulled away. As he headed for his house he wondered if he shouldn't have gone inside with her, to check to make sure Sheila hadn't decided destroying the car's fuel system wasn't enough and wanted to take it to another level.

He needed to find out more about this Sheila Price. Blaze seemed to know her and sounded hopeful they might be able to gather enough evidence to put her behind bars. How much damage could she do to Monica's life in the meantime?

Monica. The very way her name rolled through his thoughts made him

13

want to get to know her better. Such a sweet woman with the innocent qualities that brought out the protective urges within him. With an accent like that she wasn't from Montana. So, what was she doing in Blessing? It wasn't as though it was a tourist hot spot.

He pulled in front of his house and his former exhaustion seemed to be replaced with unease. Sleep might take a while to come when his thoughts were tangled up in the brown haired beauty next door. If it were any other woman, he might put the moves on her and have her in his bed before his next shift, but something about this woman told him she deserved more. She was too innocent for one of his impersonal flings, and he wasn't sure he was ready for *more*. She also lived next door which would make things all the more complicated if she ended up despising him. Even as he told himself she was off limits, his thoughts continued to find ways to bring them together. It was more than his body reacting to her, he wanted to know her as a person.

Some women have been trying for years and they were barely a blip on his radar, yet in less than thirty minutes she worked her way into his thoughts enough that he couldn't stop thinking about her. *Just my luck, the one woman who I shouldn't want is the one I do. Boy, can I pick them, or what?*

CHAPTER THREE
DINNER DATE

All day butterflies danced in Monica's stomach as she cleaned and cooked. The thought of calling off the dinner had crossed her mind a couple times throughout the day. Though she extended the offer out of gratitude it seemed too romantic to have Smoke over for dinner. Even with the doubts she couldn't back out. It was what her mother would have expected her to do. When someone went out of their way to help, she had been raised to return the favor. Her mother might have baked one of her famous apple or cherry pies, but she wasn't the baker her mother was. It was nice to cook a full meal for adults, instead of either cooking something small for herself or preparing dinner for the Day children. Coming from an influential family she'd have thought they'd be open to different foods, but what they'd eat was extremely limited. Chicken nuggets seemed to be their favorite, with spaghetti coming in a close second.

A home cooked meal with good company was what she needed after everything that was happening with Sheila. Cooking kept her busy, keeping her mind off the situation and the company would be nice. Besides spending her days with the Day children, she was sorely lacking social interactions. Adult conversation sounded almost too good to be true.

As far as she knew, Detective Wilson was still looking into what happened to her car. The mechanic who had fetched the car from the side of the road called to inform her that the gas line had indeed been cut. The line hadn't burst or been hit by a rock on a road causing the leak, it had been professionally cut with a compact cutter. Whoever had done it had crawled under the car and did it on purpose, and to her there was no doubt who was responsible. Sheila.

With dinner over and the dishes in the dishwasher the pressure seemed to disappear. There was an ease between them as they sat on the sofa in front of the gas fireplace, chatting about this and that. While they barely knew each other she found him easy to talk to. Someone she hoped to be able to spend more time with in the coming weeks, hopefully without the stress of Sheila hanging over her head.

"You're worrying again." Watching her carefully, he brought the wine glass to his lips.

"I'm not." Guilty, she couldn't meet his gaze and instead focused on her own wine glass. "Okay, maybe a little, but it seems like I should have heard from Detective Wilson by now. The mechanic called, but I don't know...I expected to hear from Detective Wilson."

"Knowing Blaze, I'm sure he's waiting until he has something certain to tell you." He placed his hand on hers which was resting on her leg. "No news might be good news. Give him time. The police department is like everyone else, they can only work so fast. I assure you it's not like the cop shows on television. Hours of work go into the smallest details of the investigation."

"For a firefighter you seem to know a lot about the police department." She stared down at their hands. The comforting touch felt right, but more than that it made her want to move closer. Images of his hands running along her body flashed within her thoughts and heat coursed through her. *What the hell am I thinking? I just met him.*

"In my line of work, we come into contact with the police a lot. I've become friends with many of the officers in the area, either through work or Blaze, and even with those I'm not, we're still friendly when we come across each other at calls. Firefighters, cops, paramedics, the search and rescues team, all of us work hard so we like to play hard. Who else better to do that with than someone who understands the demands of our jobs? The police department doesn't run on the same shifts we do, so they're not on for twenty-four hours at a time, but their job is just as demanding."

"Work hard, play hard." She chuckled. "Seems like all I ever do is work hard."

"The joys of being a nanny," he teased. "We need to change that. I think I can help you play hard if you give me the chance. Tell me, how did you manage to get off the next several days? I thought if you were lucky a nanny might manage a day or two off a week."

"Mr. and Mrs. Day are lawyers. Their practice isn't here in Blessing but they chose to live here because it gave their children a better school system and their clients wouldn't be able to find them as easy. I took the kids to their office a few months ago, because they had a family event after work, and ran into one of the people they represent. Let's just say I wouldn't want them knowing where my children lived either."

"Sounds like they care enough about their children, they want them safe." Smoke nodded.

"Not enough that they spend time with them. But it doesn't matter, it's temporary. If I don't find something before Mr. Day finds out about Sheila's threats he's going to fire me anyways. This time off is the prelude to my unemployment." She took a drink of her wine and shrugged. "To answer your question, Mr. Day is from Billings. It seems his younger brother got himself into some legal trouble. So, he's going down to represent him for the trial and they took the kids to visit their grandparents for a few days. Last time they

17

made me travel with them his parents complained. They shouldn't be paying me when the children are there to visit their grandparents and they're perfectly capable of looking after them"

"Everyone needs time for themselves. Raising someone else's children has to be a challenge."

"Challenge is an understatement. The parents are never around and because of that they let the kids get away with everything. They lavish them with gifts instead of spending time with them. The youngest is three-months-old and she's the easiest to handle, but their nine-year-old is a terror." She chuckled, thinking about all the issues she had in the last year working for them. "Enough about me. Tell me what gave your mother the idea to name her sons Smoke and Blaze? It's a little unusual to say the least."

"There's actually three of us. Blaze is the youngest. My twin, oh you're going to love this, his name is Fire."

"Smoke and Fire. You've got to be kidding me?" Trying to hold back the laughter bubbling from within her chest, she rose an eyebrow at him. "When you showed me your firefighter identification I thought Smoke was your nickname, but then I realized it was a certified ID and they'd never use a nickname. I didn't say anything at the time considering I needed your help, but it was hard not to laugh at the unique name."

"Dad was a firefighter and Mom spent many years as the president of the Ladies Auxiliary. They were dedicated to their community and the fire department so when she got pregnant it only seemed right to give their sons names that had been such a part of their lives. I'm just glad I don't have one of my cousins' names."

"Which are?" She leaned back against the sofa, her gaze on him, as she waited. There wasn't a doubt in her mind that this was going to be a good one.

"Arson and Torch."

With the wine glass near her lips she was thankfully hadn't taken a sip yet, otherwise her light blue tank top would have been covered in red wine as she choked on the liquid. Laughing so hard she had to set the glass on the end table. "Now that's worse."

"My aunt had been trying for years to get pregnant, nothing worked. My uncle was a fire investigator and he was working an arson case. It was driving him insane, long hours and more stress than he was used to. From what I've been told, and mind you I'm scarred from this, but he liked to burn off that stress in the bedroom. Seems all they needed was a little stress relief and she got pregnant with the twins. Aunt May wouldn't be left out of the tradition my mother started and that's how my cousins got their names." He polished off his wine before reaching for the bottle and refilled her glass before topping his off.

"Is it a tradition your parents are hoping you'll continue? If so, you might run out of names."

"Are you trying to tell me Backdraft, Brushfire, or Flame won't work? Mom's going to be real disappointed if the mother of my children won't agree to those. I've put real thought into coming up with the perfect names." His gaze on her and the seriousness to his face made her question if he was being truthful or teasing her. It wasn't until he cracked a smile she realized he was joking.

"Flame might work but I can only image the teasing Backdraft would go through growing up. You can't do that to your son."

"Hey now, that was going to be the name of my little girl. It will warn all the boys that messing with her will be dangerous for their health. Just like a backdraft is for firefighters," he teased. "And do you really think that Smoke, Fire, and Blaze were not teased as children? Well, at first at least. It wasn't until I knocked some little punk on his ass that the other kids realized I wouldn't put up with that crap. Say shit about me fine, but my brothers are

19

off limits. When it comes to them I'm like a furious dog. I bite."

I want to feel your teeth…shit! She took another long sip from the wine glass and wondered what was wrong with her. It wasn't like she was a virgin but to have all these sexual thoughts about someone she just met was unusual. She had dinner with men before without falling for their charm and allowing them to carry her off to bed. With Smoke it seemed like all her self-control went out the window, leaving her hot and somewhat out of control.

"From your accent I can tell you're not from around here. If it's not prying too much, what brought you to Blessing?"

"The job." His finger teased over her knuckles, drawing small circles around each one before moving to the next. "I'm from a small town in South Dakota, a country girl who grew up on a farm. I wanted to spread my wings and get away from the pressures of being the oldest child. Growing up with seven younger sisters I helped my mother raise them, so being a nanny was something I was sure I could do. My uncle is a lawyer too and he met Mr. Day several years ago and when he told me about the job, I applied. They flew me out here for two weeks to see if I'd work out and when I did, I was hired. That was more than a year ago now. See my grandparents took over the farm from my grandfather's parents and Dad took it over from them. He wants me to marry someone who will take it over from him too, but…"

"You want more," he supplied.

"Is that so wrong?" Drowning the guilt running through her, she took another drink of wine. The farm wasn't enough for her and as much as the look of pain in her father's eyes when she told him that she was leaving weighed on her, she had to do what was right for her. "My uncle was the same way. His parents wanted him to be a farmer, but he went to law school against their wishes."

"He encouraged you to follow your own dreams." He nodded as if understanding her predicament. "Do you regret it?"

Not wanting to jump to an answer she took a moment to think about it. She didn't so much miss South Dakota as she missed her family, especially her sisters. Family had been everything to her. From the time she graduated high school until she left home her days were filled with caring for her sisters, helping her mother around the house, or helping the younger ones with their homework. She was a little mother to them, leaving no time for herself or for dating. "No, I don't regret it. I miss my sisters, but other than that home is a memory."

He wrapped his arm around her shoulder, bringing her closer to him. "Good, because I'm glad you landed here."

"Me too." She tipped her head to look up at him, brushing her cheek along his shoulder. "I'm glad you happened to be on your way home from work—"

His lips claimed hers, stealing the words from her throat before she could finish the sentence. Surprised, a moan tore from her lips, opening them just enough to give him access, and he slipped his tongue between them. She wasn't sure if it was the wine or her own need that made her return the kiss. If it was the wine, she was thankful he brought it.

In the background her cell phone rang, but she couldn't bring herself to care enough to pull away. She adjusted her wine to the other hand and reached up to run her hand along his chest. The thin material hid where she wanted to be. She wanted skin touching skin, but she could feel the toned muscles under her fingers. Vibration from the pocket of his jeans had her pulling back slightly.

"It's okay, darling." Even after he broke the kiss he kept her pressed tight against him as he dug into his pocket. "It's just my cell."

"My phone..." She leaned forward, sat her wine glass aside, and grabbed it.

"My bet is it was Blaze." He held his phone toward her, showing her the display. *Missed call: Blaze.* "I'll call him and see what's happening."

"Do you think he found something?" Her hands shook, making her glad that she put down the wine. Her stomach twisted into knots, hoping for any kind of news. "Maybe he's made an arrest."

"Let's find out." He hit the button and brought the phone to his ear. "Blaze…"

She watched him, looking for any sign of concern he might have and hoping for a hint as to what Detective Wilson wanted. Smoke's gaze found hers again and his fingers pressed into her shoulder.

"Okay, I'm already at her house. Get here when you can. I'll fill her in." He hit the end button and dropped his phone on the sofa next to him. "He's on his way."

"Why? What's going on?"

"He has the evidence you needed and he thought you'd like to see the proof. There's a warrant for Sheila Price's arrest. Now we have to wait until the police locate her or she turns herself in."

His arm was still around her shoulders but his body had gone stiff, putting her on guard. "There's more though isn't there?"

"She's gone." He brought his other hand to her cheek and forced her to look at him. "Monica, it's going to be okay. They'll find her."

"Gone?" Her jaw was slack as she stared wide eyed at him, praying she hadn't heard him correctly. This was the break she had been waiting for and now it was being snatched from her because the woman had disappeared. She couldn't have just vanished, she had to be somewhere.

"Blaze and his men served a search warrant and the apartment supervisor let them in. He explained Sheila left a few hours before with a suitcase; she was supposedly heading out to be with a sick family member. Blaze has been unable to locate any living family. It's likely she knew they would trace this back to her and took off." His finger teased along the curve of her cheek. "It's

22

going to be okay."

"You don't know that. I mean…what if she knows where I live? I've tried to keep it quiet but maybe she found out."

"Then come stay with me."

"What?" Shocked, she pulled out of his embrace and rose off the sofa. The restless energy made her want to pace but her legs were like jelly making her feel unsteady.

"I don't mean in my bed, well only if you want to," he teased. "Honestly Monica, I have plenty of room and after tomorrow you'd have the house all to yourself for twenty-four hours. It will give Blaze time to catch her and you'll feel safer."

"Thanks, but I can't." She could picture her father's reaction when he heard she was staying at Smoke's house. He'd have a fit that would put the last time he had been angry with her to shame. It would be another disappointment that she could add to the list. One she didn't want to add. There was already a wall of distance between them, one she didn't want to grow further.

"Well the offer stands. Or if you'd prefer to stay here, I can crash on your sofa." He patted the sofa next to him. "Worrying isn't going to help anything. Blaze will find her. You have to trust in that."

Coming back to the sofa she nodded. She wasn't sure if it was because she believed him or because it seemed like the right thing to do. Sheila had been causing issues in her life for weeks now and there had been nothing for the police to connect her to any of it. Now with hard evidence to tie her to a crime, Sheila had disappeared. It seemed like the start of a bad horror movie, rather than her life.

CHAPTER FOUR
DISMISSED

As the days turned into two weeks without an issue, it should have relaxed Monica. Instead, it only put her more on edge. Where was Sheila? What was she planning next? All of that weighed on her mind as she slipped out of her car and headed for the front door of the Days' house. Work was one of the only things that could keep her mind off Sheila, the other was Smoke. They had grown close over the last two weeks, spending most of their mutual time off together. Even the days he was on duty, he always found time to call or text her to see how she was. Knowing he took time out of his day to check in with her was touching. Finding him when things were crazy had been the best thing that had come out of this whole mess.

With her thoughts on Smoke and their plans for the following day, she hadn't noticed Mr. Day standing on the porch waiting for her until she came to bottom step. "Mr. Day, I thought you would have already left."

"I should be at the office, but I had my schedule rearranged allowing me to be here when you arrived. Have a seat, we need to talk." He held his hand toward the two wooden rockers decorating the porch. As far as she knew they were purely for decoration, in all the time she worked for them no one had ever used them.

"I hope everything is okay with my performance." Her nerves made her fidget with her purse strap as she took a seat.

"Your performance on the job is outstanding. The issue at hand is your personal life." He held out to her a paper he had been holding. "It's come to my attention that you have a stalker. This former roommate has made threats against you and now this police report—"

"That was weeks ago." This was the moment she had dreaded since Sheila started her torture. A moment she thought had passed in the wake of Sheila's disappearance.

"Which you didn't tell me about. Rather, I had to learn it from a colleague."

"There haven't been any problems since then." She already knew where this was going but she couldn't give up her job without a fight. "Mr. Day—"

"Monica, at this time having you employed with us is endangering our children. We're going to have to let you go. I've already made arrangements with the bank to direct deposit your final check along with a severance payment into your account today." He pulled the paper back from her and rose. "I'm sorry, Monica. You've been great with the children but one day you'll understand."

"Understand?" She shot to her feet.

"Yes, you'll understand that as a parent you'll go to great lengths to protect your children. That's the same reason we moved our family here."

"Says the man who's never around. You and your wife are so busy with your careers you don't realize your children are acting out just to get your attention. They need parents in their lives, not nannies, and they certainly don't need to be lavished with gifts." Even though she expected this, anger flooded her as she stormed off the porch and back to her car.

It wasn't until she was half way to home that things began to sink in. What was she going to do without a job? Her only skills were caring for children, cooking, and housekeeping. Her parents raised her to be a wife and mother, they never expected her to be anything other than that. Old-fashioned but in her small hometown it was all too common. Now it left her wondering what her next move would be. The fear of having to return to South Dakota tightened her chest. Things were just starting with Smoke and now her future was more uncertain than ever.

For the first time in months Smoke's shift was uneventful, the calls were minimal, giving them a lot of downtime. He tried Monica a few times throughout the day, but like him she was also working and the Day children must have been keeping her busy since she hadn't returned his calls. While normally he'd be out there in the dayroom with the rest of the crew, watching television, playing cards, or just bullshitting to pass the time, he wanted some quiet time and had slipped into the sleeping quarters. Leaning back on his bunk he flipped through a magazine.

"You need to get laid." His twin brother Fire strolled toward him, his hair still wet from the shower.

"Fuck you."

"You've got your woman on your mind."

Smoke tossed the magazine onto the mattress beside him and eyed his brother. "What's your point?"

"I knew the moment you bought that house you were getting soft." Fire sat down on the bunk next to Smoke. "You and Blaze are going to leave me as the lone Wilson brother standing. Guys night is going to get mighty lonely for me."

"He's not that serious about Chrissy." At least Smoke hoped he wasn't. Blaze deserved better than her and after the last time they broke up he was certain his brother understood that. Only to find out a week later they were back together. Someday his brother would wise up, hopefully.

"I hope not." Fire dragged his hand through his short hair, sending a couple water droplets flying through the air. "But you're serious about the girl, aren't you?"

"I was just thinking about that." It had only been a few weeks but he was convinced she was the woman he had been looking for. She fit into his life like she had always been there. Before they could take things further he had to know if she would be able to deal with his career.

His first year with the department he had been in a steady relationship with his high school sweetheart. He thought they could make something work between them. Even then part of him knew it wouldn't be the happy marriage his parents had but he'd have made it work because he loved her. Or at least he thought he loved her. Later he realized what he felt for her wasn't love but lust. Everyone thought the two of them made the perfect couple, so he stayed. It wasn't until she started to despise his career that he knew he couldn't continue the farce any longer.

"Good." Fire slammed his hand down on the bed. "It's about time you got over Suzi and from what Blaze tells me this Monica is an amazing woman. She's strong and isn't breaking under the pressure of this bullshit going on. When am I going to meet her?"

"Soon."

Alarms blared in the sleep bay area, bringing Smoke to the upright position. Every time that alarm went off it sent a burst of energy rushing through him. Every call was different and he never knew what to expect, especially at night. Something about the darkness and fire had always excited him.

They rushed out of the sleeping quarters and headed toward the bay, as dispatch stated the call details. *House fire…seven-forty-one Hamilton County Road.* "Fuck."

"Hey Smoke, isn't that your road?" Jay hollered at him as they climbed onto the engine.

"Yeah…it's my neighbor's house." As they zoomed down the streets, heading toward home and his woman he couldn't get his mind in the game. Monica. *Shit, darling, please be okay.*

CHAPTER FIVE
INFERNO

A screeching noise woke Monica from a dead sleep on the sofa and sent her to her feet in a split second. She tried to place the noise but the fog that had come from being rudely awakened made her brain slower. Coughing, she blinked; it had been dark when she fell asleep but now...

Fire! The orange and red flames lit the house in an all-consuming glow. Beyond the squeal of the fire alarm that had woken her, the hiss and pop could be heard as the fire burned the wooden frame of the cabin. Grabbing her purse from next to the sofa, she tried to find the door. *I've got to get out of here.*

It was hard to see through the heavy smoke and it took her two steps in the wrong direction to realize her bearings were off. She turned around she glanced down the hall toward the bedroom, only to see flames dancing up the walls through the thick smoke. Fear spiked within her as she realized the house was engulfed. Flames licked up the living room walls, making the smoke thicker. Everywhere she looked all she could see was the orangish-red glow of fire. She was surrounded. Standing there would leave her dead in a matter of minutes with the way the fire was spreading. With no other option she forced herself to move.

Reaching the door, she reached out and grabbed the handle, only to have the scorching metal burn into her palm, forcing her to let go before she could open it.

Slipping her purse strap over her head, so that it crossed over her body, she looked for another way out. The thick smoke made it hard to breathe and she tried to remember what she learned as a child. The only thing that came to mind was stop, drop, and roll.

"Damn stop, drop, and roll is if I'm on fire." How hadn't her parents taught her anything to do in this kind of emergency situation? They taught her everything else she might ever need in life. Yet in that moment she seemed so very ill prepared for this.

"How do I get out of here?" As if to answer her question, sirens blared. *Smoke!*

Unable to take the smoke any longer she lowered herself to her hands and knees and made her way over to the window. The fire was growing in size and between the smoke and the heat from the blaze suffocating her she wasn't sure how long she'd last. Did she have time to wait for the rescue squad? Or should she continue to find a way out? Terrified if she moved away from the window they wouldn't be able to find her, she stayed put. *Please let them get here in time.* Darkness closed in on her, but if she passed out, she'd die. She fought to stay conscious, to keep fighting to live.

The door exploded inward, sending chunks of wood in every direction. On hands and knees she inched closer to the door, desperate for fresh air. Through the smoke a figure emerged. From the light of the flames she could make out a firefighter, beyond that she didn't care. A split second beyond, another firefighter entered, ax in hand. "Monica!"

Coughing, she crawled toward them, the heat intensifying around her. *Just a little further…fresh air…* Someone hauled her into his arms; through the gear and face mask she couldn't see who it was.

"I got her." It sounded like Smoke but the muffling from the face mask made it hard to hear him.

"Paramedics are standing by," the other firefighter said as she was carried out.

"Wilson, get another line." Through the smoke she couldn't tell where the voice came from, but it sounded far enough away it must have been near the fire truck.

Wilson? Smoke are you here?

"Go on, brother, I've got it." The second firefighter who rescued her jogged toward the fire engine.

Her thoughts circled those words. *Wilson? Which one? Does that mean Smoke or Fire is the one carrying me?* If it was Fire she was making a mighty fine first impression.

"Let me down…" A coughing fit overcame her again and he raised her in his arms slightly. "I can walk."

"Not a chance, darling." Ignoring her demands, he headed toward the ambulance.

So grateful to be alive, she hadn't bothered to look closely at her rescuer. Now with the only light being the flames of her cabin, she tried to look through the gear, to the man behind the mask. "Smoke." The single word brought tears to her eyes. He came for her.

"Shh darling, you're safe now." He eased her onto the gurney before he squatted down in front of her and took his breathing mask off.

"Is this the woman you were talking to Fire about earlier?"

"Shut up, Sam and help her." Smoke eyed the paramedic for a moment before returning his gaze to her. "Blaze is on his way and I'll be back soon. I've got to help the guys get the fire under control."

"Go. I'm fine." She put her hand up, stopping Sam from putting the oxygen mask over her face. "Thank you."

"I'd always come for you." He kissed her forehead, rose, and headed back to the other firefighters battling the blaze.

"My home…" she mumbled more to herself than anyone else as Sam placed the oxygen mask over her mouth. Sitting on the gurney, unable to do anything as her cabin turned into a pile of rubble, she was overcome by anger and sadness. *Sheila.* There might not be proof *yet*, but part of her knew they'd find it in the rubble.

"Things can be replaced. What matters is you're alive. Now lie back and let me look at your hand. Are you burned anywhere else?"

Doing what he asked, she watched Smoke and the others. This was what he did and while she realized the dangers of it before she was never so grateful as she was at that moment. He saved her life. They all did in a way. It might have been Smoke who picked her up and carried her out of the fire, but they were all responsible for her being alive. If he hadn't been on duty, there wasn't a doubt in her mind one of the other guys would have risked themselves to do the same thing. It wasn't just because it was their job. No one would risk themselves day after day, shift after shift, for a job they didn't love. If there were any reservations about his work before, they were gone. Maybe he was the man he was because of the job and there wasn't a chance she was going to change that. She was falling in love with him. The conversation with her mother only days before flooded back into her thoughts, stealing her away from the moment at hand. Needing the escape, she let her eyelids drift shut and darkness claim her, as her mother's voice ran through her thoughts.

"You're in love."

"What?" The spoon fell out of Monica's hand and clattered onto the counter. "Mom…"

"Monica." Her mother's tone cut her off, making her remain silent. "I'm your mother and I've been where you are. I can hear it in your voice so there's no use denying it. I have

twenty minutes until your sisters get home, so tell me about him."

"There's not much to tell." She pushed the empty bowl of ice cream aside and leaned against the counter, her gaze quickly finding Smoke's house off in the distance. "He's a good man. Honest, trustworthy, kind, a man Dad would like."

"But?" Her mother pressed when she grew silent.

"It's happening too quick. I just met Smoke a few weeks ago and now…" Unable to look at the house any longer, she turned away from the window.

"Now, you're in love."

"Mom…" Even as she tried to defend herself, she couldn't keep the smile off her face.

"I bet you don't know that your father and I only knew each other for five months before we got married. Six weeks after we met he asked me to marry him and I said yes. Love at first sight isn't just in those romance novels you used to read so much. It happens and when it does you've got to embrace it."

"What was the rush to get married?" She couldn't help but ask the question. Had her mother been pregnant with her when they got married? The time frame would have worked out because she knew her parents hadn't even been married for a year before she was born.

"To answer your unasked question, no I wasn't pregnant with you. You didn't happen until our honeymoon. We got married because we were in love, not because of a premarital pregnancy. I'm only trying to tell you that when you're in love, time doesn't matter. For your dad and me it felt like years instead of months. We couldn't picture spending a single day apart."

She understood what her mother was saying because that's what she felt like with Smoke. He had only been in her life a few weeks but there was a connection she hadn't felt with anyone else. "Thanks, Mom."

"So, when do we get to meet him?"

"Monica."

Her eyelids sprang open and she found Blaze standing at her side. "Detective Wilson." Bright lights shined overhead. "Where am I?" She started to rise but the oxygen line running to her nose pulled tight, stopping her.

35

"What's going on?

"It's okay. You're safe." On the other side of the hospital bed Smoke leaned closer, placing his hands on her shoulder. "Just lie back."

The sight of Smoke with his turnout gear still on and soot marring his cheek, brought everything rushing back to her. Her house, the fire, and him saving her. "How did I get here? I was getting oxygen…my house was on fire."

"You lost consciousness after Sam put the oxygen mask on you. Moments later you were loaded into the back of the ambulance which brought you here." Smoke took her uninjured hand into his, squeezing it gently as if to reassure her. "You're okay though. The burn on your hand isn't too bad. It's going to hurt for a few days, but things could have been a lot worse."

Their gazes locked and in that moment all she wanted was to crawl into his arms and forget everything that happened, but Blaze was there. She needed to know why. Had he found something? She knew in her heart Sheila was responsible but could Blaze prove it? "Why are you here?" Her mother would have scolded her for being ungrateful and unwelcoming, but the words were out before she could stop them. "Sorry Bla…Detective Wilson."

"Please call me Blaze. It would seem as though we should at least be on a first names basis." His gaze shifted to Smoke before back to her. "I came to deliver good news; Sheila Price has been arrested."

"Arrested?" She tugged the oxygen line off and leaned forward. "For what? Destroying my car? What about my house?"

"Excuse me." An older man with just a touch of gray mixing into his dark hair and a white lab coat entered, looking between the three of them before landing on Blaze. "I won't have you upsetting my patient."

"Doctor Cobb, I only need another minute of her time," Blaze informed him.

"The nurse said she was fine and you'd be discharging her." Smoke's back straightened as he watched the doctor. "Did you find something..."

"Are either of you family? Otherwise without her permission—"

"Is there something wrong with me?" Alarm rang through her and for an instant she forgot about Blaze's announcement that Sheila had been arrested.

"You inhaled some smoke and there's a burn on your hand but other than that you're in perfect health," Doctor Cobb assured her. "It's hospital policy that our patients are not disturbed while they're here. Undue stress can make the healing process take longer."

"I'm not stressed. Trust me, he's brought me good news. Now can I leave?" If anything, they were relieving some of the stress that had been weighing on her for days.

"I'd like to keep you overnight for observation."

"And I'd rather not." She slipped her hand from Smoke's, pulled back the tape and pulled the IV from her hand before anyone could stop her. "I want to go..." Go where? She didn't have a home. A night or two in a hotel would be all she could afford now that she was out of work. The idea of returning to South Dakota soured her stomach.

"Don't worry, Doc, I'll keep an eye on her." Smoke rose to his feet and placed his hand on her shoulder, bringing her attention back to him. "You'll come home with me."

"What about work?" She didn't know what time it was, but she didn't figure too much time had passed, which meant he was still on duty. "Wait, why are you here? Not that I'm not glad you're here but I mean, shouldn't you be at the station?"

"Captain sent me home. Hell, I refused to even go back to the house and change." He took her hand into his again. "I was coming for you with or without his permission."

"It's against medical advice but it seems like you'll be in good hands. I'll

37

have the nurse bring the paperwork in." With another look at Smoke and Blaze, Doctor Cobb nodded, and left.

"Well that's taken care of, I guess I should get back to work." Blaze grabbed his suit jacket from the hospital chair and turned to leave.

"Wait. You didn't tell me what happened."

"Sheila Price arrived back at the apartment you two shared and told her new roommate what happened between you two and that she burned down your house with you inside. According to the witness, her words were something along the line of 'this is what happens when you fuck with me'. She believes you deserved this for moving out of the apartment, she has no idea what she's about get in return; prison. I bet she'd have thought twice about it if she knew what kind of time she was looking at." Blaze cracked a grin.

"How did you find out she was back at her apartment?"

"She didn't do much research on the new girl. Otherwise she'd have known that she's a paramedic and her fiancé is an officer with the Blessing police department. She called it in, evidence was gathered, and an arrest was made."

"I can't believe it." She stared at Blaze in shock, as if waiting for him to say it was some kind of cruel joke.

"Believe it." Blaze shot her a grin as he slipped his suit jacket on. He glanced at his brother before lowering his gaze back to her. "My brother is hard to live with, a complete pain in the ass, but he'll fuck up anyone who messes with those he loves. If you can put up with him, more power to you, but if he gets to be more than you can bear, give me a call and I'll knock him down a peg or two. Now get some rest, I'll be in touch."

"Umm…thanks I guess." She gave him a grin. "I don't want it to go to his head, but he's a pretty good guy. One I'm lucky to have in my life."

"Give it your best shot, little bro." Smoke shot him a cocky grin.

With only a shake of his head, Blaze headed for the door.

"It's over, darling." Smoke squeezed her hand.

She watched as Blaze strolled from the hospital room, leaving her alone with Smoke. "Over but it's too late."

Too late for my house, my job, my chance at staying here…with you. It's all over before it even really started.

CHAPTER SIX
FARMHOUSE

Smoke's house wasn't anything like Monica had expected. The old farmhouse had been completely remodeled, bringing it into the present while keeping the details and charm of the house. The kitchen was her favorite with a large open area and plenty of counter space. The island with the bar stools for anyone who might be in the kitchen while someone was cooking, reminded her of home. Many of her memories growing up involved sitting around the kitchen with her mother and sisters. They'd spent so much time there that it was more comfortable to her than even the living room. Becoming homesick, she forced herself to move past the memories and continue to take in the rest of the space.

The dark cherry wood cabinets looked original to the house, adding character, while the light granite countertop was new and added enough contrast to make it stand out. To separate the kitchen from the living room he had added deep red barn doors onto a sliding track that could be closed whenever he needed them, and while they were open, they made the two rooms feel like one large open space.

"You're supposed to be resting."

She turned and found Smoke standing in the doorway in cotton shorts and a Blessing Fire and Rescue shirt. "I'm...sorry, your house wasn't what I was expecting. I shouldn't have started exploring but couldn't sit."

"All I meant is you've gone through a lot tonight. The doctor gave me strict orders to have you resting and you're not supposed to be alone." Inside the kitchen he grabbed a beer from the fridge and leaned against the counter. "I'd offer you one but with the pain medication you shouldn't drink. There's plenty of other things to drink if you're thirsty, just give me the word. How's the hand feeling?"

"I'm good and my hand's fine too." She looked down at her bandaged hand and while it didn't hurt right then there was no doubt it would be miserable over the next few days. The palm of her hand had been burned badly but considering her home was a complete loss it could have been a lot worse. If she hadn't woken up when she did, she could have died. *If it wasn't for Smoke I would have.* "Thank you."

"For what?" He twisted the cap of his beer bottle.

"Coming for me." When he opened his mouth to say something she cut him off. "I know I said it before but..."

He stepped away from the counter and went to her. "But what?"

"I guess I realized how close I came to dying. It must not have been enough for Sheila to just torment me any longer, she must have wanted me dead. No wonder Mr. and Mrs. Day let me go. I put their children at risk by being near them. You're in danger because of me..." She leaned back against the counter and tried to stop her thoughts from wondering what she was going to do next. Going home could put her family at risk. She couldn't risk her sisters.

"Hey now, darling." He sat his beer down on the counter and wrapped his arms around her waist, pulling her against his body. "It's going to be okay. We're going to get through this. Sheila's behind bars and Blaze is certain he has a strong enough case against her that she'll be going to prison for a long time. He's hopeful she'll confess and there's a possibility of her taking a plea deal. If she does you won't have to deal with a trial or anything. You can start to put this behind you."

She wanted to believe him but her thoughts were going a mile a minute and wouldn't be diverted from the path they were on. "Bringing the police into this might have made her grudge against me worse. What happens when she gets out of jail? If she's not convicted, it could be sooner rather than later. If she is, that could make the hatred she has for me stronger. I'll put everyone around me in danger. My family…"

"Are in South Dakota and they're safe. This isn't about them. Her rage is at you, not them."

"I have to go home." The announcement felt like a lead weight had hit her in the stomach. Leaving was the last thing she wanted to do. It had only taken a few weeks for things to progress with Smoke. What was happening between them was special and the thought of leaving him behind made her sick. They had something happening between them and as much as she was scared to admit it she was falling in love with him. South Dakota was the last place she wanted to go.

"Why?" His gaze stayed locked on hers. She took him in, searching for some idea as to what he was thinking, but she couldn't even find the smallest hint.

"You might have missed it but my house is a nothing but a pile of rubble and burned framing." She tipped her head toward the window above the sink, directing his attention toward what was left of her cabin that was in view on the other side of the trees. "No house and no job kind of makes it hard to stay here. I burned through my savings to rent that place and now it's gone. Now…"

"Now you're going to stay here with me." He squeezed her tighter to him. "It's a large house, plenty of room. There's a guest bedroom down the hall from me you can take over."

"Is that where you want me to stay?" She ran her hand up his chest. The urge to take their relationship to the next level resurfaced within her. This time she wasn't willing to deny it. Before her nerves always got in the way. Not tonight. Maybe it was how close she came to dying or the thought of losing him. Tonight, she wanted nothing to stand in the way.

"Darling..." His hand ran down her back, gently caressing her as he worked his way down toward the hem of her shirt. "Where would you like to stay?"

"Would it be too forward if I said in your bed?"

"Exactly where I want you." He grabbed his beer, took another long drink, before setting it aside and tipping his head down to her.

Looking up at him, their gazes met, and she nodded. "Let's go upstairs."

"I can't think of anywhere else I'd like to be." He scooped her into his arms and headed for the stairs. "Tonight, when I heard the address of the house fire my heart stopped. Every second I spent in that engine seemed too long. Like it was taking us twice as long as it should have to get to you. Still none of that compared to what I felt when I saw you through the window."

"You saw me?" She hooked her arm around his neck as he climbed the stairs.

"Yes." He looked down at her, letting their gazes linger on each other for a moment. "Flames all around you and for the first time in my career I was terrified we wouldn't get to you in time. I was ready to rush in but Fire stopped me, forcing me to take a moment for my gear. I was suited up but I needed to pull my breathing apparatus on. Good thing it's second nature now because you were all I could think about. I wanted to get you out of there, to get you somewhere safe, so I could..."

"What?" she pressed as he laid her on the bed in the master bedroom—his bedroom. She took hold of his hand, keeping him there, because something in his gaze made her believe he was going to step back from her. "Smoke…"

"I want you, Monica. I want you so bad it hurts. To know you were next door instead of my bed was driving me crazy." He tugged his shirt over his head and tossed it on the floor next to the bed. "When we have a hysterical woman or an irate man, I make one of the other guys deal with it or Sam. Emotions have never been my forte. I can never come up with the right words. What I'm trying to say is that I'm in love with you."

"Come here." She leaned up on her forearm and held out her other arm to him. He came to the edge of the bed but didn't sink down to sit next to her. She took his hand in hers, interlacing their fingers, as she gently tugged him down toward her. "I had a very similar conversation with my mother a few days ago."

"Really now?" He raised an eyebrow at her.

"Mom and I have always been close and she could hear the change in my voice. It took a few minutes of her nagging before I told her I was falling in love with you and it terrified me."

"Why, darling?" Finally, he dropped down onto the bed next to her. The desire and love that was in his eyes only moments before was now replaced with doubt. "My job?"

At the question hanging in air she realized his career had been an issue in previous relationships. For her it wasn't a problem. His job brought him to her when she needed him the most. "No." She squeezed his hand, hoping to convey the truth of her words in the simple gesture. "We've only known each other a few weeks. I thought it was too quick to have such strong feelings for someone. We've been together almost every day, unless you're on duty. Still it seemed too quick."

"And now?"

"Now." The corners of her lips curled up into a smile. "The feelings I have for you don't scare me. I know I want you and that's what matters."

"Well then." He rose from the bed and quickly stripped off his shorts and boxers, leaving him standing naked before her. "I think I can give you what you need."

Her gaze scanned down his body, taking in the defined muscles and tanned skin. Her fingers ached to run along his chest, to feel every chiseled aspect of his toned body and to explore every part of him. "I think I'm overdressed." She slipped the shirt Smoke had given her to wear over her head and tossed it toward the foot of the bed.

"I think I can help you with that." He reached behind her, unhooked her bra and stripped it from her in one clean move. "Let's forget about Sheila and everything else. Tonight is about us."

"Us." It came out as a whisper as she slid her hands along his chest. Even though she wasn't sure what tomorrow would bring, she liked the way that sounded.

He sat down on the bed next to her, his arms wrapped around her waist. He kissed her, a long, slow deliberate kiss that gave and demanded. He cupped her breasts and teased the nipples, gently swirling his thumb against the hard buds before pinching them. Pain mingled with pleasure and she arched into his body. He abandoned her mouth and he kissed her neck, nibbling down her jawline to her shoulder. Slowly he teased kisses down her chest until he came to her breasts and his tongue flicked over her hardened nipple. The pleasure forced a moan from deep within her as she arched toward him. It felt as if every nerve ending in her body was alight with desire. The simplest touches fanned the burning desire within her. Looking up at her he sucked the nipple into his mouth, allowing his teeth to run along either side, before he allowed the hardened bud to slip from his lips.

"I love how your body responds to me." He slid into bed next to her, his hand teased along the curve of her hip, coming to the hem of her black panties. "These have got to go."

Without pants on they were the last thing standing between them and in one quick wiggle she rose up enough to slip them off and kicked them off the bed. His gaze traveled over her body, taking all of her in. Nervous, she wrapped her arms around herself.

"Don't." He took hold of her hands, placing them at her sides. "I want to see every beautiful inch of you."

As if to prove that, his hand slid down her body and between her thighs. The caresses of his fingers had her spreading her legs and her breath caught in her chest. Sliding his hand up her inner thigh ever so slowly until he could slip his finger between her folds, quickly finding her center and working deep within her. She moaned as he added a second finger. In and out, quicker with every pump. As her climax approached he slowed, until he stopped all together.

Even as she wiggled against him, wanting more, he took his time. Easing his way back up the length of her body he blazed a trail of kisses across her stomach, stroking his fingertips along the curves of her sides. With every touch, she arched her hips into him, demanding more. Yearning coursing through her, she could wait no longer for him to claim her. Her mind was in a sexual haze, needing him now.

"Not yet, darling."

"Please, Smoke," she moaned, arching toward him.

"Soon." He pressed his lips to her neck, dragging his teeth along the smooth skin before leaning back.

She reached down and ran her fingers through his hair. "I want you, rough and full of heat, until we're both out of breath. It seems like I've waited months for this moment. I want you now."

"Why don't you set the pace?" He rolled over onto his back, waiting.

"I didn't expect you to give up control that easy." Her gaze scanning along his body; she loved how at ease he was naked before her. Not that he had anything to want to hide. He had a body that showed he worked out. Her on the other hand, she had aspects she wanted to change. Maybe if she took the time to hit the gym she'd have the confidence he had.

"I like to be the one in charge but tonight is all about you. Beautiful, are you up for the challenge?" Grinning at her he put his arms behind his head and waited.

Not wasting a moment, she straddled his hips and wrapped her hand around his shaft. Gliding caresses up and down the hard length, she teased his erection harder. He groaned and reached up to caress her breasts. Heat coiled between her thighs and her core clenched.

"I've waited so long for this moment." She loved the feel of him in her hand and knowing she caused his shaft to be rock hard.

"Then let's not waste another second." Even with his suggestion, he did nothing to urge her to move faster.

Desperate, she shifted her position and angled the head of his shaft just below her opening and sank down onto it. Slowly allowing his hardness to fill her, easing in inch by inch as her body adjusted to his width, until his low moan echoed hers. Moving his arms from behind his head, he reached out and pinched her nipple, the pain mingling with pleasure spurring her on as she rocked upward and then down again, finding her rhythm. Impatience coiled through her as she tried to find the right motion. As if realizing her frustration, he grasped her hips, increasing his pace and driving up into her with force.

With every thrust, his pace sped, his hands on her hips pulling her down onto him harder and faster. Stroke after stroke, the tempo between them intensified until his hips where slamming off hers. The thrusts became deeper and faster, falling into a perfect rhythm. Their bodies rocked back and forth and her back arched, pushing her breasts out toward him as her orgasm neared. The tension strained through her muscles, tightening around his shaft.

"Fuck, darling." His fingers dug into her hips. "Do that again. Tighten your muscles around me."

As she pushed down onto him, he arched up to meet her. Faster and deeper, they met each other's thrusts. They climbed the mountain, both seeking the apex.

"Smoke!" Screaming his name, she slammed down onto his body as her orgasm found her. Her nails dragged along his chest, leaving angry red scratches.

His grasp on her hips tightened, keeping his shaft buried deep within her as his own orgasm hit him. "Fuck, Monica." The desire and need in his voice tightened her chest. "I could get used to this."

She collapsed on top of him, her hands on either side of him, holding him tight to her. This had been what she had wanted. She went to bed each night thinking about this very moment. Now that she was in his arms and his bed, she was afraid it was too late. If she couldn't find a job soon she'd have no choice but to return home to South Dakota. "I'm sorry, I'll get off you."

"No, darling." He wrapped his arms around her, holding her in place. "You can stay there all night if you wish."

"Then let me enjoy my after sex bliss." She wrapped her lips over his nipple, gently biting it.

"Fuck, Monica." His cock twitched inside of her, sending a jolt of desire rushing back through her, forcing her inner core muscles to tighten around him again. "Darling, if you do that again, I won't be responsible for my actions."

"What will you do?"

"I'll roll you over and fuck you until you're so sore you can't walk straight tomorrow, let alone sit." He swatted her ass, making her jerk in surprise.

"Smoke!" she squeaked as she slipped off him to lie next to him. His arm wrapped around her, pulling her close until her body was pressed up against his. In that moment, cuddled against him, her life felt complete. The idea of waking up next to him every morning and having amazing sex like this every night brought a smile to her face. She finally understood what her mother had been saying before and she wanted to claim what was happening between them with both hands. "I love you, Smoke."

"I love you, too." His hand slid down her arm, as he turned his head to look at her. "I don't know what I would have done if I hadn't gotten to you in time."

"You did, that's all that matters," she reminded him. He was her rescuer and the holder of her heart.

CHAPTER SEVEN
OPPORTUNITIES

It was well after nine in the morning when Smoke's eyelids fluttered open and it took him a moment to remember what happened. He was supposed to be waking in his bunk at the station. Instead he found himself at home, with Monica snuggled against him, still asleep. He pressed his lips to her forehead and she looked up at him.

"Morning." Her voice was soft and full of sleep.

"You're even more beautiful in the morning." Under the blanket he traced his finger along the curve of her hip, fighting the urge to pull it back so he could see every inch of the naked body pressed against his. He rolled toward her, his hard shaft teased along her thigh.

"I'd like nothing better than to spend the day in bed with you but I can't and you know if you start that now we'll never get out of bed." Even as the words came out she slipped her hand between them, her fingers teasing along his hard shaft.

"Darling, that's dangerous territory unless you want to end up flat on your back."

"I can't…" Her fingers wrapped around it, sliding up and down the length. "I've got to call my parents. I've got to…" Her hand stopped before she could finish sliding down the length of him.

"What? You've got to what?"

"Make reservations to go back home." She spit the words out without meeting his gaze.

"Is that what you want?" His hand stilled on her hip as ways to convince her to stay with him raced through his thoughts. Now that he had her in his bed he wanted her to stay there. The thought of losing her was like a knife to the gut.

"What I want? Hell no, but that doesn't matter."

"Why?"

"Could we have this conversation once we're both dressed?" She tried to pull back from him. Not willing to let her go, his arm tightened around her waist.

"You chose the time to bring it up, so let's finish it." He pressed his forehead to hers. "Plus, darling, I'm planning on making love to you once I convince you to stay."

"If it was only that easy."

"It can be if you let it." He brushed her hair away from her face. "You said it yourself last night. You want to stay here, you want to see where things will go, so why are you making reservations to go back to South Dakota?"

"Mr. Day fired me yesterday. I'm out of work. I've been tired of the Day children and have been looking for work for weeks now, but there's nothing here in Blessing. Any job openings I've found online requires me to leave the area. If I have to leave, I might as well go back to South Dakota. My skills are limited and the only work history I have is with the Day family. Now that they've fired me…"

"What if I could secure a job for you? Would you stay?"

"A job?" She raised an eyebrow at him but didn't give him time to answer. "There's still the issue of my house."

"Bullshit." He rose up onto his elbow. "We discussed that last night as well. I want you to stay right here. There's a guest room if you'd prefer but I think you made your desires known. You want to be right here in my bed just as much as I want you here."

"Dad's going to have a fit when he learns I'm staying with you."

"From what you've told me about your parents, I suspect you're right. I also believe he wants you to be happy and safe. You're happy here in Blessing, aren't you?"

"Happy since I found you." She ran her hand along his chest. "Before you I was questioning my decision to leave home. With the crap going on with Sheila and hating my job I felt like my only option was to go home."

"Now new doors are opening for you." He reached up and cupped her cheek. "Sheila is behind bars, the Day children are no longer your responsibility, and you can do anything you want. If you want to continue with what you know and care for children I know someone who is looking for someone."

"Who?"

"Scarlet, she's a paramedic at the station. She's a single mother and needs someone to care for her daughter while she's on duty. Best part is our shifts are the same, so our schedules would work together. She has two weeks of maternity leave left." His thumb teased along the curve of her cheekbone. "Let me give her a call, we can meet later today, and you can see. She's a doll and you're going to love her little girl. Even if you don't want to work with her or kids anymore, you can find something else. I want you to stay."

"I promised I'd visit my parents soon. It's been a year since I've been home, and my sisters are complaining. They want to meet you too…"

"Is that an invitation?" He pulled her tight against him. "Because I'm pretty sure I convinced you to stay and you invited me home to meet your family."

"I guess so." She nibbled on her bottom lip with her gaze staying on him.

"Things are moving fast between us but if I'm staying here with you then my dad is going to want to meet you. It's either we do it there or the family descends on us here. I'd rather go to them. We can set how long we'll be there. It's the better option because if they come here who knows how long they'd stay."

"Let's talk to Scarlet first. No use in upsetting your parents with the news about the Day family if you can get another job lined up. Then we'll make reservations to go see them. Perhaps next week?"

"Next week?" Her eyes widened.

"It might be easier before Scarlet's maternity leave ends, that way she won't have to find someone else to watch her daughter while we're away." He pressed his lips to hers for a quick kiss and leaned back to look at her. "You pick the days and I'll make travel arrangements."

"Last minute flights are expensive."

"Unless you have a buddy with a plane who owes you one. Now come on, let's get some breakfast and I'll call Scarlet. Otherwise your naked body is going to be too tempting and I'm not going to be able to keep my hands off you." He slid his hand down her body, as if tempting her to stay into bed.

"Then come on." She slipped out of bed before he could change his mind and pull her back against him. "There's plenty of time for sex. Right now, I can think of a hundred things that need to be done. I need to check to see if my car got damaged with the fire last night or not."

"We'll check it out after breakfast." He got out of bed and quickly began to dress.

"Good because I need to get some clothes and other things." She tugged on the same jeans she wore yesterday. No doubt they smelled like smoke, but she didn't have anything else. Quickly slipping into her bra and the Blessing Fire and Rescue shirt he'd given her to wear, she turned back to him. "I can cook while you call Scarlet."

"You just want to get out of here before I push you back on the bed, strip those clothes off you, and make love to you again." He grabbed a shirt and tugged it over his head. "Because darling, you know I would. It's nearly impossible to keep my hands off you."

"Resist the urge until you've fed me." She chuckled and strolled out of the master bedroom as he grabbed his cell phone.

"If you give me ten minutes I'll help prepare breakfast. Let me get in touch with Scarlet first."

"Don't worry. I promise I won't burn the house down," she hollered over her shoulder as she headed downstairs.

"Don't worry, darling, I'd save your ass again. I guess it's handy to have a firefighter around." He chuckled to himself as he pulled up Scarlet's number. It had been a few days since he'd seen Scarlet and she mentioned she still needed to find someone to watch Hannah while she was on duty. Her parents didn't live close enough to do it and while her sister offered, she had her hands full with her own kids. It was up to Scarlet to find someone responsible enough to handle caring for a newborn infant during her twenty-four-hour shifts. At the time Smoke hadn't known Monica was looking for another job or he'd have recommended her in an instant. If he knew anyone who could handle the responsibility it was Monica.

One day it will be my child...our child...she's caring for. The idea of being a father never held so much interest as it did at that moment.

CHAPTER EIGHT
FUTURE

Breakfast was over and dishes were done but they had time to kill before they had to leave to meet Scarlet. Knowing no better way to spend the time they had to wait than making love to the woman he loved, Smoke came up behind her and wrapped his arms around her. "Come on darling, staring out at your house isn't going to make it rebuild."

"I only lived there a few weeks but it's sad to see the first place I lived alone reduced to nothing but rubble. Mr. Butler called me while I was cooking breakfast, he doesn't want to rebuild. He's going to sell the land." She leaned back against his chest, her gaze still out the window.

Holding her, he made a mental note to give Mr. Butler a call to see about purchasing the land. He never considered himself sentimental before but the idea of someone besides Monica living over there didn't sit well with him. He wanted to purchase the place years ago because at one time the land had belonged to this farm house. The family before him had been forced to sell it off in order to keep their home. In the end it hadn't mattered, they lost the house, and it gave him an opportunity to purchase it cheap.

"Come on darling, let me take your mind off of all of this." He kissed along her jawline until he reached the sweet spot below her ear. Grazing his teeth over the area, he blew his cool breath against her flushed skin.

"First tell me why there's a height chart in the pantry door." She turned slightly in his arms to look up at him. "You got a couple kids I don't know about hidden away in the basement?"

"No, the family I purchased the home from." He tugged his shirt up her body until she grabbed the hem of it and pulled it over her head, dropping it on the floor. "It's their kids. When I was remodeling I couldn't remove them. It seemed like part of the house, so I left it. It's the history of the house and while I renovated to bring the place current, I didn't want to destroy the history of this place. The details here are something I love, which is why I purchased it. Plus, there's plenty of room beside it for us to have our kids' height chart next to it."

"That's sweet. All I could see were initials. I couldn't make out much. If I thought this place had been your childhood home I would have figured it was your height chart, but you said you purchased it a few years ago." She moaned in pleasure as he nibbled and kissed his way down to her breasts.

"Enough talking. I'm going to make you scream my name."

"Really now. Is that not talking in a way?" she teased. "Over the last few weeks I can't tell you how often I've thought of this. Of you."

He slid his hand around her body, quickly finding the clasp of her bra and unhooking it. The material slid down her arms, revealing her perky breasts, making his shaft strain against his shorts, and pressed her against the counter. Her words barely registered through the fog of desire. All he knew is that he wanted her right there in the kitchen. Maybe they'd make it their mission to have sex in every room of the house, to make this place theirs in every way.

Claiming her nipple with his teeth, he gently tugged, making it hard before moving over to the other one. Without breaking contact, he unhooked her jeans. "We should be doing this in the bedroom. To have you sprawled out on my bed again, naked and wanting."

"The bedroom is overrated." She rose up, tugging her jeans down the curve of her butt. "Back up and let me get out of these."

He stepped back, giving her space to kick off her jeans while he took care of his own clothes. In a flash they were naked and he closed the distance between them.

"You're more beautiful than I remember."

"I grew more beautiful in the hour since you saw me naked?" She shook her head at him. "Somehow I doubt that."

"Hiding your amazing body behind clothes makes me forget how incredibly sexy you are. I think I want you naked all the time."

"That will work well around other people. You wouldn't be jealous or anything." Teasing, she looped her arms around his neck, pulling him back toward her. "And I'm sure my parents will approve."

"Are you mocking me, darling?" He tweaked her nipple. "You're right. I don't want you naked around anyone else but me. How about on my days off we spend the whole time in bed, naked together?"

"The pleasure filled forty-eight hours after every shift might leave us both exhausted, but as long as you feed me once in a while I'm up for that."

"Good, because I don't know if I can get enough of you." He gripped her hips, easing her toward the edge of the counter, crushed his mouth to hers, and slid his hand between her legs. Unerringly finding her core, he thrust his fingers into her and she moaned around his unrelenting kiss. He held her captive against his body, teasing her clit with his thumb. Fierce desire had her rocking against his hand. She was ready for him.

"I want you," she murmured against his mouth, her nails digging into his sides as she arched into him.

His teeth grazed her lower lip and he pulled his hand away. Her cries of frustration only confirmed the climax he felt building within her, but he ignored her demands. "Darling, the way your body is reacting you would think I've been neglecting you. I can feel your muscles clenching around me as you seek your orgasm. Maybe I should make you wait."

"Cocky bastard. Keep messing with me and I'll leave you high and dry." She grabbed his hips. "I've gone through a burning hell—literally—don't you think I deserve a little compassion?"

"Compassion? Is that what they're calling it these days?" He adjusted his angle, gliding his shaft over her opening, pulling a moan from her. Slowly he glided the length of him in, just a little at first, her nails digging into his back as he worked his way inside her tight passage. Halfway in he stopped and slid out, even as she clung to him trying to force him to stay.

"Smoke…please, I need you."

"I know, darling." Once he was out, he gripped her hips and slammed his length into her, filling her completely. He didn't give her time to catch her breath and began rocking their bodies back and forth, each thrust gaining momentum.

He left her mouth and kissed a path to her neck. She pressed herself tighter against him, matching him thrust for thrust until she was bouncing off the counter. He quickly adjusted, sliding one hand under her butt, lifted her, and spun around to press her against the wall. With her secured between his body and the wall, she wrapped her legs around his hips, the heel of her foot digging into him so he couldn't pull back too far. Rather than pulling away, each thrust was faster and deeper than the last.

In this position, her chest was pressed against his and he lost the view of her breasts bouncing as he thrusted into her. A small price to pay to have himself buried deep within her, but he'd remember it next time. He longed to claim her nipple with his mouth, to tug it between his teeth as he hammered himself into her.

"Faster, Smoke!" she cried out, her nails clawing into his shoulders.

Tension had her muscles constricting around him as her orgasm neared. She leaned into him, every pump of his hips sending pulses of pleasure exploding through him. In his arms, she came apart at the seams as her climax rippled through her and he continued to drive into her, her moans echoing off the walls. He pushed into her again before his own ecstasy had him exploding within her. His moans mixed with hers until he dropped his head into the curve of her shoulder, planting gentle kisses along the nape of her neck.

"Wow." Her voice was low and breathless, making his shaft, still buried deep within her, twitch with new life. "That was—"

"Amazing? The best you ever had?" he offered, lifting his head from the curve of her neck to look at her.

"Okay." Her lips curled up into a smug smirk. "I can't have you getting a big head or anything."

"Most definitely not." He arched into her again, letting her feel every inch of him. "Want me to show you how amazing it can be again?"

"Later." She leaned against him. "I'm going to be sore if we keep up at this pace."

"We can't have that, especially not until after we meet with Scarlet." He grabbed hold of her hips, lifting her up off his shaft, and helped her stand on her feet. "Whenever you're ready we'll head out and pick up some of the things you need before heading to Scarlet's."

"What about my car?" She reached over and grabbed their clothes off the floor before placing them on the counter and digging through them to find her bra.

"We can look at it before or after. Your choice."

"Before. I can't take a job with an infant without a car, anything could happen."

"You wouldn't have to." He cupped the side of her face. "Remember we're in this together. You could drop me off at the station or Scarlet and I could carpool, and you can use my truck. This bullshit with Sheila is a bump in the road. We'll get through this."

"Are you always so optimistic?"

"It's the only way to be. If you always look at the negatives in life, which there are plenty, then you're going to be miserable. Looking at the positives helps you live a happier life. Happiness is what I want in my life, don't you?"

"You standing there naked makes me want other things, but yes happiness is good." She slipped his shirt back over her head. "It's kind of sad to say but even with everything that has happened I've never been this happy before."

"Me neither, darling." Still naked, he pulled her back into his arms. "I'm glad you've decided to stay." The idea that she had considered going back to South Dakota was like a lead weight in his stomach. She was the woman he'd been waiting for and now that she was in his arms he wasn't about to let her go.

Never picturing what the future had in store for him, he was surprised by the plans running through his head. *Soon, she'll have a ring on her finger and my last name. Not long after we'll have a few kids.*

CHAPTER NINE
EXTENDED FIREFIGHTER FAMILY

It had been a long time since Monica had held a newborn baby in her arms but it all came back to her as she rocked Scarlet's daughter, Hannah. The four-week-old little girl was adorable with sparkling green eyes and a full head of reddish-blonde hair. She was the spitting image of her mother. Holding the little girl reminded Monica of all the newborn moments with her sisters. Her time being the little mother to her sisters had prepared her to be a mother to her future children one day, but it also prepared her to be a stand-in parent for those who hired her.

"Other mothers tell me Hannah is an easy baby, but there are moments when I seriously doubt that. She can be fussy at night, not wanting to go to sleep."

"I think all babies have moments like that." She looked up at Scarlet and took in the dark circles under her eyes. The woman was exhausted. Being mother and father to her young daughter with no one to rely on seemed to be taking a toll on her. "My mother always said the first few weeks after the baby were the hardest. Eight hours of sleep were a thing of the past."

"Tell me about it." As if on cue, Scarlet yawed. "Everyone tells me to sleep when Hannah does but if the sun is out I have a hard time sleeping. I purchased black-out curtains and hung them the other day but now I think I'm so exhausted that I'm not tired."

"Neglecting yourself won't do either of you any good." She glanced down at Hannah and then back to Scarlet. "You've worked with Smoke for a couple years. Do you trust him?"

"Yes, with my life." Scarlet looked from her to Smoke and then back to her. "Why?"

"Let us take Hannah for a few hours and you can get some sleep."

"Oh no, I couldn't do that. I couldn't impose." Scarlet sat up from where she had been leaning back against the sofa. Exhaustion weighing down her eyelids.

"It's not imposing. You're considering hiring me to watch your daughter. This will give me time with her and give you time to get some sleep. Smoke can supervise."

"Scarlet, she's got a point." Smoke spoke up from where he was leaning in the doorframe. "You're exhausted. We're used to dealing with sleep deprivation on duty, but this is different."

"This is on me." She dragged her hand through her reddish-blonde hair and looked from Monica to Smoke. "I chose to go through with the pregnancy, to keep her instead of giving her up for adoption like my parents wanted. She's my responsibility."

"You're not alone, Scarlet." Smoke pushed off the door frame and came to squat in front of her. "We're all behind you and this little girl is going to have a station full of aunts and uncles. No one is ever going to hurt her. Just wait until she's dating."

"Dating." Scarlet let out a deep chuckle. "I can't even think about tomorrow and you want me to think about years down the road."

"You know I'd never let anything happen to Hannah." He took her hand in his, rubbing his thumb over her knuckles. "We're family. It doesn't matter what role you play at Blessing Fire and Rescue, we're family, all of us. You also know I would never recommend someone to watch after Hannah unless I was certain she was perfect for the job. Monica is that person. She'll keep your little girl safe and will take good care of her."

"I know, which is why she's hired. That's if she wants the job." She looked over at Monica. "We'll work out the arrangements. I'm sure you'd like to stay at your own place instead of here and that's fine with me. I can bring Hannah to you before my shift."

"I…um…"

"She's staying with me," Smoke explained. "So, if you want to bring her to the house, or for Monica to pick her up that works. Everything she'd need is already there."

"What?" Monica asked, confused. "Hannah would need a crib—"

"Trust me, you have more at Smoke's place than here." Scarlet gave her a quick nod. "Then it's settled, you're hired. I go back to work two weeks from yesterday. I'm not breastfeeding, I know it's better for her but I thought it would be easier with my work schedule."

"There's no reason to explain. She's your daughter and that means you get to raise her how you want." She looked down at the little girl in her arms. "Thank you, I mean for hiring me. She's precious and I'll take good care of her while you're working."

"Smoke speaks very highly of you, so I have no doubt. He's a good judge of character, even if he can be a pain in the ass sometimes." Scarlet grinned at Smoke before looking back at her. "He's a good man but let me know if I have to kick his ass for you."

"I don't think that will be necessary but thank you." She thought about the words that Blaze told her before he left the hospital. *My brother is hard to live with, a complete pain in the ass, but he'll fuck up anyone who messes with those he loves. If you can put up with him, more power to you, but if he gets to be more than you can bear, give me a call and I'll knock him down a peg or two.*

"We have to stick together and watch out for each other. Like Smoke said, we're family. From what I can tell he's dragging you into this family of misfits. While it can sometimes put the most dysfunctional family to shame, there's no other family I'd rather belong to."

"Speaking of family." Smoke rose from before Scarlet and moved to the chair off to the side. "Monica and I are going to visit hers in South Dakota. I work the day after tomorrow but after my shift we're going to take off to visit them. We'll only be gone a couple days, four at most, because I only took the following shift off. We'll be back before you're back to work."

"Meeting her family. That's a big step." Scarlet's gaze shifted to Monica, her face serious. "Are they ready for him? Have you told them about his career?"

"They know about him and that he's a firefighter."

"Good, because I've seen that come between couples in the past. If you're okay with it and you're not going to have to take any shit from your family, then that will make things easier." Her gaze landed on her daughter. "My parents hated that Hannah's father was a police officer."

"Was?" She couldn't stop the question from slipping out. Not knowing any back story on Scarlet or Hannah, she figured it had been a fling but the picture over the fireplace with Scarlet and a man in a police uniform kissing made her wonder if there was more.

"He was killed in the line of duty." Scarlet looked over at the picture above the fireplace. "It was his last shift before our wedding. A Thursday night, two hours until he was off the clock, and we were supposed to get married that Saturday. He was responding to a domestic abuse situation when next thing I hear over the radio, *shots fired, officer down*. I was on duty and the nearest ambulance to the call. I didn't know it was him."

"Scarlet…" Smoke reached back over and placed his hand on hers.

"Don't do this."

"He's right. I'm sorry, I didn't know."

"He didn't even know I was pregnant." Scarlet's gaze lingered on the photo. "He'd have made a wonderful father. See now why I couldn't give her up? No one understood but it would be like losing him all over again. With Hannah, I still have a part of him."

"I understood," Smoke reassured her. "I think most of us understand."

"My parents didn't." With tears in her eyes Scarlet let out a deep sigh and leaned back against the sofa again. "She's all I got."

"And you're all she has," Monica reminded her. "So once again, I'll suggest you let us take her for a few hours and you can get some rest. I have to do some shopping and then we'll go back to Smoke's house. Whenever you wake up you can give him a call and we'll bring her back. Even if you want us to keep her all night. You need some rest."

"I could use some sleep." She nodded. "Are you sure you don't mind looking after her for a few hours? Smoke, is she committing you to something you'd prefer not to deal with?"

"We don't mind," he reassured her. "Hannah will be no problem and you need some rest. We'd gladly keep her for the night but are you ready to be away from her that long?"

"No, not all night. I don't know how I'm going to do it when I go back to work. But a few hours would be great." Scarlet chuckled. "Just a couple uninterrupted hours of sleep. That sounds like Heaven to me. I swear every time I fall asleep she knows and it's her cue to wake up. If I've gotten more than an hour of sleep at once it was a miracle."

"Well, get her stuff ready and I'll get her car seat out of your car and move it to my truck." Smoke stood from the chair he was sitting in and grabbed her keys off the coffee table.

"Actually, there's a second car seat in the nursery." When Smoke stopped

67

moving toward the door Scarlet explained. "Working twenty-four hour shifts makes it likely whoever had Hannah would need to go out sometime during that time. So, when they were on sale, I picked one up. I thought it would be easier for the babysitter to have one for her own car, instead of swapping it in and out of my car all the time. Just put it in your truck and then Monica can have it for hers."

"Having two does make things easier." Monica nodded. "If you get me a list of her formula, diapers, and everything else I can pick some up instead of you packing it every time. Since we'll stay at Smoke's place, I'd like to keep some extra clothes on hand for her as well. Babies can be messy and I'd hate to make her hang out all naked if I have to wash her clothes."

Scarlet threw her head back and let out a deep laugh. "My little girl is just like her father. She hates clothes. If she had a choice she'd be naked. She fights me every time I have to change her."

"Do you like to be a naked baby?" She ticked Hannah's stomach, bringing a smile to the girls' face. "Well then, clothes can be optional, but diapers are a must. There's only so many times in a day I want to be peed on," Monica joked.

"That has yet to happen to me but I have no doubt she'll manage to do it, probably right before I leave for work, especially if I'm running late."

"Little boys love to do it the moment their diapers come off. You quickly master the art of changing a boy's diaper." Monica loaded Hannah into the car seat that Smoke brought out and tucked a blanket in around her. "I don't have any brothers, but my aunt has three little boys and I've had enough experience with them to know you don't take any chances with them when it comes to changing time."

"I was worried I'd have a son. What do I know about raising little boys?" She reached over and ran her finger along the side of her daughters' face. "At least with a little girl I kind of knew what to expect. I mean, after all I was a little girl at one time."

"I think you're doing a great job with her."

Scarlet stuffed some diapers, clothes, and formula into the diaper bag as her gaze shifted back to Monica. "I just wish I didn't have to leave her. I feel like somehow by leaving her I'm letting her down."

"You're not." Monica met the other woman's gaze. "Nowadays it takes two incomes to support a family. The mother doesn't have the opportunity to stay home with the child, putting more children in daycares or with nannies and babysitters. There's nothing wrong with that as long as you're still there for your child, which I know you will be. Daycares can be a great way for your child to interact with other children. In the nanny situation, I make sure that those in my care are still interacting with other children, through playgrounds, classes, or even at the local park. I also work with the children as they grow up to prepare them for school. Their early childhood development becomes as much my responsibility as their parents', because when the parents are home they want to spend time with them that isn't about reading, learning their colors, shapes, or any of that."

"That's why I've hired you." Scarlet sat the diaper bag aside. "You have experience which is great and you were upfront with the situation that happened with your ex-roommate. I know Blaze, he's a good man. I'm confident he's handling it and you won't have any more issues. When it came down to it you were the best candidate. I'm a single mother and while I would love to do it all on my own and be a miracle worker, there's no way I can. With your help I know my daughter will be in good hands and will be where she needs to be. You're more than a babysitter and with you I know Hannah won't be neglected in anyway, not just physically but also mentally and emotionally."

"Hannah will be in good hands."

"Thank you." Scarlet wrapped her arms around Monica, bringing her in for a tight hug.

"You're welcome." As the women embraced, Smoke strolled back into the room, a grin stretched across his face.

"Now ladies, if there's something going on between you two, do I get to watch?"

"Did I mention he's a pig?" Scarlet chucked as she stepped back and shook her head. "You and Fire always have sex on the brain. You better not influence my daughter."

"She's four-weeks-old. How can I influence a baby who doesn't have a clue what the hell is going on?" Smoke grabbed the diaper bag and slung it over his shoulder. "And how come I'm always the guilty party?"

"Because you're the man," Monica offered. "Women are innocent."

"Hah." He reached down and took hold of the car seat handle, lifting Hannah and her seat up. "How about we go and let Scarlet sleep for a few hours? I mean, unless you two ladies want to have a bonding session and I take Hannah out to spread my bad influence? Maybe I could take her to a bar or strip club? I'll bet the women at a strip club would love that."

"Aren't you just a barrel of laughs." Monica shook her head before turning back to Scarlet. "Sleep until you wake up. Don't set an alarm. Whenever you're ready, give Smoke a call and we'll bring her back home."

"Thanks." Scarlet looked from her to Smoke. "Both of you."

"You're welcome. Now don't worry, she's in safe hands, just rest." Before she could reply, Monica motioned for Smoke to lead the way and within minutes they were out of Scarlet's small two-bedroom apartment and buckled in Smoke's truck.

"I don't think I've ever seen Scarlet take to someone as quickly as she took to you." He put the truck in gear and reached over to lay his hand on her leg. "You put her at ease, letting her know Hannah will be safe with you."

"That's what parents need. Their children mean everything to them, some more than others." She glanced back at the car seat, only to see Hannah sleeping soundly. "I could tell Scarlet needed to know Hannah would be safe. I was concerned when I brought up the situation with Sheila, I thought it would put me out of the running for the job, but she had the right to know. Sheila could get out of jail and come back after me. If she found out where I lived once, it won't take long for her to find out where I'm at now. It not only puts you at risk, but it puts Hannah and even Scarlet in danger. I don't like knowing my issues could affect so many others."

"I told you she's going to be behind bars for years and everything is going to be okay." He squeezed her thigh. "You have to trust me, trust Blaze, and trust in the system."

"I trust you." She did, but it was more than just that. Things had to work out because she wasn't willing to give up her life here in Blessing and she wasn't willing to leave Smoke behind to go home to South Dakota. This is where she wanted to be. She wanted to be with him.

CHAPTER TEN
MEETING THE ROBINSONS

A private plane was the way to travel but even in the comfort and privacy of the small airplane, Monica couldn't stop her stomach from somersaulting. It wasn't from the turbulence or the fact she was thousands of feet off the ground, it was because within an hour they'd be at her parents' home. Days of preparing for this trip had left her uneasy and nervous. What if they didn't like Smoke? What if he didn't like them? How would her sisters react to a strange man in the house? All the questions circled within her thoughts, making her sick.

"Monica."

Her thought bubble burst as her name drew her back to reality and she glanced over at Smoke. "Huh?"

"You're worrying for nothing." He squeezed her hand. "Everything is going to be fine."

"You don't know my father." Her stomach tightened. "I'm his first little girl…he's protective." That was an understatement, but it was the best way she could describe her father to him.

"As he should be." He pulled her off the small sofa next to him and up into his lap. "Listen to me, everything will be fine. We've already spoken with both of your parents and we told them everything that was happening. They know we're together and that you're living with me. Your dad isn't thrilled about us living together, but he's not going to have a fit when we show up together."

"What about when we leave for the hotel together?" She leaned into his embrace and rested her head on his shoulder.

"Your sister moved into your old room and there are no guest rooms. There are too many kids and not enough bedrooms. This is the best situation and you explained it to your mom yesterday when you spoke with her." He smoothed his hand along her back. "If you want to stay at the house, I understand. I'll miss snuggling next to you, but I do understand. I just don't feel comfortable putting your family out. I don't want to force your sisters to double up, so I can use their bedroom."

"Are you sure you just don't want an escape from my family? Or maybe you want me in your bed at night and you know Dad wouldn't allow us to share a room together because we're not married?"

"Maybe a little of the second one." He looped his arms around her waist. "After sleeping with you every night lately, I want to have you in my bed every night. When I'm on duty my bunk feels lonely and I can't wait to get home to you."

"Let's not tell my dad about that, okay?" She could only imagine how that conversation would go with her father. The best outcome she could come up with was him not dropping over dead from a heart attack or not killing Smoke. All the other scenarios were disastrous.

"Okay but it's going to be hard to keep my hands off you."

"Keep it PG until we're at the hotel." She turned to straddle him, so that her legs were on each side of him. "But until we land—"

The loudspeaker overhead crackled to life. "If you could return to your seats and buckle up, we're about to begin our descent. Your rental car is waiting for you on the tarmac. I hope you enjoyed your flight."

"How does a firefighter know a millionaire with his own pilot and plane? One who happens to owe you a favor."

"Family friend." He waited as she slipped out of his embrace and returned to the seat next to him. "Eli grew up down the street from me but we weren't very close. A couple years ago his family home caught on fire and his sister and mother were stuck in an upstairs bedroom. I rescued them and since then we've gotten to know each other a little better."

"Because you saved his mother and sister, he lent you his plane and pilot." She shook her head.

"Something like that. I explained the situation and he helped a friend in need. Getting you home to see your family after everything that happened was important. He's close to his family, especially since the fire, so he understood what this visit would mean to you. With your new job watching Hannah, time was limited."

"Thank you." She leaned into him and he wrapped his arm around her shoulders. "Even though I'm stressed about how Dad's going to handle our relationship, I needed this trip home. After all the shit with Sheila, I really needed to reconnect with my sister and my mother."

"I know, darling."

"I think I might be able to make this up to you later." She ran her hand down his leg, teasing along the inside. "Just wait until we're back at the hotel."

"We have a little time now. Why don't you—" The plane touched down onto the tarmac, stealing the rest of his words. "Shit."

"The mile-high club will have to wait until our return trip."

Moments later they were descending the stairs from the private plane when the doors from the airport opened and her mother and father strolled toward them. "Shit."

"Darling?" His hand slipped into hers, not understanding her remark

75

until his gaze found her parents as well. "What are they doing here?"

"My parents no doubt wanted to meet you before my sisters. I'm sorry." She squeezed his hand.

"Don't be." He grabbed their suitcase from the baggage attendant and pulled the handle up so he could wheel it across the tarmac.

"Monica!" Her mother jogged toward her. "It's been too long."

"I've missed you, Mom." She let go of Smoke's hand and wrapped her arms around her mother.

"Thank you for bringing my little girl home." Her father held his hand out to Smoke. "It's been too long since she's been home."

"My pleasure, sir." Smoke and her father finished shaking hands as she let go of her mother.

"Dad, I've missed you." She stepped between them, before her father could question Smoke. "What are you guys doing here? I told Mom we'd check into the hotel and come to the house."

"This hotel issue—"

"Dad, please don't."

Smoke placed his hand on her shoulder, gently rubbing it.

"I don't like it." Her father shook his head, as he eyed both of them.

"I know, Dad, but it's easier. Jacey took over my room and let's face it you don't have room for us at the house." Her stomach twisted. This was a fight she really didn't want to have with her parents, especially not at the airport, with people watching them.

"We have room for you at the house. Let him go to the hotel." Her father eyed Smoke. "A man who respected you would want you at the house instead of in a hotel with him."

"All due respect, Mr. Robinson, but I respect your daughter." Smoke let his hand fall off her shoulder and stepped to her side. No longer was she between them as they stared each other down. "It's her decision as to where

76

she'd like to stay and before we arrived she decided to stay at the hotel. If she'd like to stay at the house with you, I understand."

"Very well then, the decision is made; she'll stay at the house."

"No, Dad, I won't." She slipped her hand into Smoke's and met her father's gaze. "We're staying at the hotel together."

"Harry…" Her mother tried but her father waved his hand, cutting her off for a moment before she gathered the courage to continue. Normally in their household her father's word was law and her mother never spoke out of turn. "Monica is an adult now. You know they're living together and staying in the hotel together is no different. Let's just be happy our daughter is home. Even if it's only for a few days."

"I don't like it." Her father shook his head.

"I know, Dad, but I'm not a little girl anymore. I love Smoke and I want to be with him."

"Remember when we were young and in love," her mother chimed in again.

"I would have never bedded you before we were married," he snapped at her.

"Times have changed, Harry."

"Please, let's not fight about this. I want to have a few days home without the constant stress that this could bring." She wanted to look back at Smoke, to gather courage from him, but kept her attention on her father.

"Let's head back to the house and get some dinner. Your mom and sisters have been cooking up a storm since early this morning." He turned on his heels and headed back into the airport.

"Don't worry, Monica, I'll deal with your father. Go on to the hotel, check in, and hurry to the house." She squeezed her hand and hurried after her dad. "It's so good to have you home again."

"Well, that went better than I expected." Smoke squeezed her hand before he nodded toward the car. "Come on, let's go to the hotel and freshen up before we head to your house."

"As long as we make it quick. I don't want Dad thinking we're having an afternoon quickie." She chucked as she opened the passenger side door. "Who knew coming home would be so stressful. I'd almost rather deal with Sheila again than to face my father's anger about me staying at the hotel."

"You did, darling." He placed their bag in the trunk before coming around to her side of the car, his hand on the door. "Don't worry; the rest of the visit is going to go better. Now get in." She slid into the passenger seat and he shut the door before coming around to the other side and climbing in.

She wasn't convinced but didn't argue with his hopefulness. Someone out of the pair needed to be optimistic and it sure the hell wasn't her.

Even though Smoke told Monica the visit would get better and there wouldn't be such tension lingering in the air, he hadn't been sure. It wasn't until the following day and a conversation with her father he'd realized the two of them wanted the same thing. They wanted Monica to be happy. While her father had wanted her to marry someone who would one day take over the family farm, he also realized it wasn't what she wanted. She had gone to Blessing a young naïve girl and had come home a woman. He was beginning to realize that and unfortunately, for her sisters, the dream of one of them marrying someone who would take over the family farm was passed onto them. Harry was hoping it would be Jacey, but Smoke wasn't sure she was any more of a fit than Monica had been. That was a piece of information Smoke was keeping to himself. He might share it with Monica but there wasn't a chance he was going to clue Harry in on it.

Strolling through the meadow behind her family's home, Smoke couldn't help but notice the ease within her. She seemed to be at peace and the weight of everything that happened with Sheila was gone. This visit with her family had done her good, too bad it would end the next day. He had to get back for his shift and there was still cleaning she wanted to do on the nursery that had been fully furnished when he purchased the house. She wanted everything perfect before Hannah's first night at Smoke's house.

"You're lost in thought." She let go of his hand and spread out the blanket, so they could sit and look out over her father's farm. "Care to tell me about it?"

"Actually, I do." Realizing this was the perfect moment he pulled out the ring box from his pocket and dropped to his knee in front of her. "From the moment I saw you moving into your house, I knew there was something special about you. The night I found you walking along the side of the road at one in the morning I knew I wanted to get to know you better. Now that I have, I don't want to let you go. You're the woman I've been waiting for all my life. I love you, Monica Robinson. Will you do me the honor of being my wife?"

"Yes." She dropped down onto her knees in front of him and wrapped her arms around his neck. "I love you too, Smoke. I want to spend the rest of my life with you."

"Good because if not, I'm pretty sure your father was going to make you move out of my house," he teased and slipped the ring on her finger.

"You didn't ask me because of him. Did you?"

"No, darling." He sat down on the blanket and pulled her into his lap. "I've wanted to for days now, but I wanted to do it right. I waited until we were here, so I could ask your father's permission. We spoke this morning while he was showing me around the farm and ever since I came back I've wanted to pull you away from your family and ask. Since we're leaving tomorrow I didn't want to interrupt your time with them. When you asked if I wanted to take a walk, I figured this was the perfect moment and then this…"

He held his hand out at the view. "This is where you grew up, this is home, and it's beautiful here. It was the perfect place."

"You could have asked me at the worst possible moment and I would have said yes. I love you, Smoke, and I want to spend the rest of my life with you." She snuggled up against him and glanced down at her ring. "But this…this moment, everything about it, including you asking my father for my hand, it was perfect. Thank you."

"Just wait until our wedding day. I'm going to make sure it's the wedding of your dreams." He wrapped his arm around her, holding her tight against him.

"As long as you're the man at the end of the altar that's all I need." She let out a lighthearted chuckle. "Well and my family there because we'll never hear the end of it if we elope."

"You set the date and we'll fly your family in on Eli's plane. Your sisters will love that." He'd do anything to make his girl happy and her family was part of that. Even though her father had issues with him at first, Smoke believed they'd overcome them with time. He was marrying Harry's little girl and eventually they'd give her parents grandbabies. "We need a baby."

"Those take time. I can't give you one tomorrow. Unless we can borrow Hannah."

"I guess I should have said I want us to have a child. Not tomorrow but soon. You're amazing with Hannah and with your sisters. I want one of our own, well more than one, don't you?"

"Yes." She leaned back against him. "I love kids and being a mother is important to me."

"Then you better pick a wedding date soon because if you end up pregnant before we walk down the aisle your dad might kill me and when we get back to the hotel I want to start practicing." He nuzzled her neck. "Practicing is the fun part."

MARISSA DOBSON

Born and raised in the Pittsburgh, Pennsylvania area, Marissa Dobson now resides about an hour from Washington, D.C. She's a lady who likes to keep busy, and is always busy doing something. With two different college degrees, she believes you're never done learning.

Being the first daughter to an avid reader, this gave her the advantage of learning to read at a young age. Since learning to read she has always had her nose in a book. It wasn't until she was a teenager that she started writing down the stories she came up with.

Marissa is blessed with a wonderful supportive husband, Thomas. He's her other half and allows her to stay home and pursue her writing. He puts up with all her quirks and listens to her brainstorm in the middle of the night.

Her writing buddy Pup Cameron, a cocker spaniel, is always around to listen to her bounce ideas off him. He might not be able to answer, but he's helpful in his own ways.

She loves to hear from readers so send her an email at marissa@marissadobson.com or visit her online at http://www.marissadobson.com.

ALSO BY MARISSA DOBSON

Alaskan Tigers:

Tiger Time

The Tiger's Heart

Tigress for Two

Night with a Tiger

Trusting a Tiger

Alaskan Tigers Box Set Vol. 1

Jinx's Mate

Two for Protection

Bearing Secrets

Tiger Tracks

Healing the Clan

Alaskan Tigers Box Set Vol. 2

Her Black Tiger

Tiger Trouble

Alpha Claimed

Roaring to be Claimed

Forever Creek Shifters:

Forever's Fight

Protecting Forever

Crimson Hollow:

Romancing the Fox

Loving the Bears

A Lion's Chance

Swift Move

Purrable Lion

Bearly Alive

Saved by a Lion

Furever Mated Box Set

SEALed for You:

Ace in the Hole

Explosive Passion

Operation Family

Marine for You:

Lucky Chance

Back from Hell

A Marine's Second Chance

Tanner Cycles:

Until Sydney

Phantom Security:

Different Sides

Undercover Agent

Takeover Agent

Cedar Grove Medical:

Hope's Toy Chest

Destiny's Wish

Leena's Dream

Cedar Grove Medical Box Set

Fate:

Snowy Fate

Sarah's Fate

Mason's Fate

As Fate Would Have It

Half Moon Harbor Resort:

Learning to Live

Learning What Love Is

Her Cowboy's Heart

Half Moon Harbor Resort Vol. 1

Stormkin:

Storm Queen

Blessing Montana:

Smoke

Touch of Home

United Homefront Ranch:

Destination Heaven

Beyond Monogamy:

Theirs to Treasure

Reaper:

Touch of Death

Clearwater:

Winterbloom

Unexpected Forever

Losing to Win

Christmas Countdown

The Surrogate

Clearwater Romance Volume One

Small Town Doctor

Stand Alone:

SEALed Rescue

Past Comes to Light

SEALed in Texas

Starting Over

Secret Valentine

Restoring Love

www.ingramcontent.com/pod-product-compliance
Lightning Source LLC
Chambersburg PA
CBHW020637130626
46552CB00003B/1276